WONDER

THIS JOURNAL BELONGS TO:

Be the wonder you want
to see in the world.

love

D0122003

CHOOS
KIN

"HERE'S WHAT I THINK: THE ONLY REASON I'M NOT ORDINARY
IS THAT NO ONE ELSE SEES ME THAT WAY." —AUGGIE

"WHAT KIND OF PEOPLE ARE WE? WHAT KIND OF PERSON ARE YOU?
ISN'T THAT THE MOST IMPORTANT THING OF ALL? ISN'T THAT THE KIND OF
QUESTION WE SHOULD BE ASKING OURSELVES ALL THE TIME?"
—MR. BROWNE

"I LOVE THAT FEELING WHEN YOU FIRST OPEN YOUR EYES IN THE MORNING AND YOU DON'T EVEN KNOW WHY EVERYTHING SEEMS DIFFERENT THAN USUAL. THEN IT HITS YOU: EVERYTHING IS QUIET." —JACK

"SHALL WE MAKE A NEW RULE OF LIFE . . . ALWAYS TO TRY TO BE A LITTLE KINDER THAN IS NECESSARY?" —J. M. BARRIE

"I DON'T WANT TO BRAG OR ANYTHING, BUT I'M ACTUALLY CONSIDERED SOMETHING OF A MEDICAL WONDER, YOU KNOW." —AUGGIE

"THERE ARE ALMOST ALWAYS MORE THAN TWO SIDES TO EVERY STORY."
—MR. TUSHMAN

"I WISH EVERY DAY COULD BE HALLOWEEN. . . . THEN WE COULD WALK AROUND AND GET TO KNOW EACH OTHER BEFORE WE GOT TO SEE WHAT WE LOOKED LIKE UNDER THE MASKS." —AUGGIE

"HOW WONDERFUL IT IS THAT NOBODY NEED WAIT A SINGLE MOMENT
BEFORE STARTING TO IMPROVE THE WORLD." —ANNE FRANK

"THIS YEAR THERE SEEMS TO BE A SHIFT IN THE COSMOS. THE GALAXY IS CHANGING. PLANETS ARE FALLING OUT OF ALIGNMENT." —VIA

"THE GOOD THING ABOUT LIFE . . . IS THAT WE CAN FIX OUR MISTAKES SOMETIMES. WE LEARN FROM THEM. . . . ONE MISTAKE DOES NOT DEFINE YOU." —JULIAN'S GRANDMÈRE

"WHAT WISDOM CAN YOU FIND THAT IS GREATER THAN KINDNESS?"
—JEAN-JACQUES ROUSSEAU

"I THINK WHEN PEOPLE DIE, THEIR SOULS GO TO HEAVEN BUT JUST FOR A LITTLE WHILE. LIKE THAT'S WHERE THEY SEE THEIR OLD FRIENDS AND STUFF, AND KIND OF CATCH UP ON OLD TIMES. BUT THEN I ACTUALLY THINK THE SOULS START THINKING ABOUT THEIR LIVES ON EARTH, LIKE IF THEY WERE GOOD OR BAD OR WHATEVER. AND THEN THEY GET BORN AGAIN. . . . THEY GET ANOTHER CHANCE TO GET IT RIGHT. . . ." —SUMMER

"SUCH A SIMPLE THING, KINDNESS. SUCH A SIMPLE THING." —MR. TUSHMAN

"THE THINGS WE DO ARE . . . LIKE THE PYRAMIDS THAT THE EGYPTIANS BUILT TO HONOR THE PHARAOHS. ONLY INSTEAD OF BEING MADE OUT OF STONE, THEY'RE MADE OUT OF THE MEMORIES PEOPLE HAVE OF YOU." —AUGGIE

"NOT ALL THOSE WHO WANDER ARE LOST."
—J. R. R. TOLKIEN

"YOU ARE MY EVERYTHING. YOU UNDERSTAND ME, VIA? *TU ÉS MEU TUDO.*"

—GRANS

"WHAT THIS WORLD NEEDS IS A NEW KIND OF ARMY—
THE ARMY OF THE KIND." —CLEVELAND AMORY

"LIFE IS AHEAD OF US. IF WE SPEND TOO MUCH TIME LOOKING BACKWARD,
WE CAN'T SEE WHERE WE ARE GOING." —JULIAN'S GRANDMÈRE

"SOMETIMES IT'S GOOD TO START OVER." —JULIAN

"I KNEW HE COULDN'T EXPLAIN HIS PLUTONIAN TEARS." —CHRISTOPHER

"KIND WORDS DO NOT COST MUCH. YET THEY ACCOMPLISH MUCH."
—BLAISE PASCAL

"I DON'T KNOW IF [WE] FOUND EACH OTHER BECAUSE WE WERE SO ALIKE
IN SO MANY WAYS, OR THAT BECAUSE WE FOUND EACH OTHER,
WE'VE BECOME SO ALIKE IN SO MANY WAYS." —VIA

"LEARNING WHO YOU ARE IS WHAT YOU'RE HERE TO DO." —MR. BROWNE

"BE KIND, FOR EVERYONE YOU MEET IS FIGHTING A HARD BATTLE."
—IAN MACLAREN

"FUNNY HOW SOMETIMES YOU WORRY A LOT ABOUT SOMETHING AND IT TURNS OUT TO BE NOTHING." —AUGGIE

"I FELT THE PART. I UNDERSTOOD THE WORDS I SPOKE.
I COULD READ THE LINES AS IF THEY WERE COMING FROM MY
BRAIN AND MY HEART." —MIRANDA

"I STARTED LAUGHING, NOT EVEN BECAUSE I THOUGHT HE WAS BEING THAT FUNNY BUT BECAUSE I WASN'T IN THE MOOD TO STAY MAD ANYMORE."

—AUGGIE

"A DREAM IS LIKE A DRAWING IN YOUR HEAD THAT COMES TO LIFE."

—CHARLOTTE

"WE CARRY WITHIN US THE WONDERS WE SEEK AROUND US."
—SIR THOMAS BROWNE

"YOU'D LOOK UP AND SEE A BILLION STARS IN THE SKY . . . LIKE SOMEONE
SPRINKLED SALT ON A SHINY BLACK TABLE." —AUGGIE

"PERFUME AND TIME MAKE EVERYTHING EASIER TO BEAR."
—JULIAN'S GRANDMÈRE

"I WANT TO BE IN LOVE LIKE THAT SOMEDAY." —VIA

"I REALLY BELIEVE . . . THERE ARE MORE GOOD PEOPLE ON THIS EARTH THAN BAD PEOPLE, AND THE GOOD PEOPLE JUST WATCH OUT FOR EACH OTHER AND TAKE CARE OF EACH OTHER." —AUGGIE'S MOM

"I'M NEVER GOING TO BE ONE OF THOSE GROWN-UPS THAT USE
AN UMBRELLA WHEN IT'S SNOWING—EVER." —JACK

"I WASN'T USED TO SEEING SO MUCH SKY IN EVERY DIRECTION. . . . I COULD UNDERSTAND WHY ANCIENT PEOPLE USED TO THINK THE WORLD WAS FLAT AND THE SKY WAS A DOME THAT CLOSED IN ON TOP OF IT." —AUGGIE

"KINDNESS IS DIFFICULT TO GIVE AWAY BECAUSE IT KEEPS COMING BACK."
—MARCEL PROUST

"THE LAUGHTER I HAD INSIDE JUST POURED OUT OF ME." —AUGGIE

"YOU DON'T NEED YOUR EYES TO LOVE, RIGHT? YOU JUST FEEL IT INSIDE YOU. THAT'S HOW IT IS IN HEAVEN. IT'S JUST LOVE, AND NO ONE FORGETS WHO THEY LOVE." —AUGGIE'S MOM

"GRANDMÈRE JUST TOLD DAD HE HAS A BRAIN LIKE A CHEESE SANDWICH."
—JULIAN

"WE CARRY WITH US, AS HUMAN BEINGS, NOT JUST THE CAPACITY TO BE KIND, BUT THE VERY CHOICE OF KINDNESS." —MR. TUSHMAN

"I KNEW FROM THE MOMENT I SAW HER." —JUSTIN

"I HELD ON TO THAT SECRET AND LET IT COVER ME LIKE A BLANKET." —VIA

"PLUTO WAS OUR TATOOINE." —CHRISTOPHER

"IT'S NOT ENOUGH TO BE FRIENDLY. YOU HAVE TO BE A FRIEND." —CHARLOTTE

"A MONUMENTAL SHIFT. A SEISMIC SHIFT. MAYBE EVEN A COSMIC SHIFT. WHATEVER YOU WANT TO CALL IT, IT WAS A BIG SHIFT." —AUGGIE

"HOPEFULLY, A LITTLE MOUTHFUL OF KINDNESS TODAY MAY MAKE THEM HUNGRY FOR A BIGGER TASTE OF IT TOMORROW." —MR. BROWNE

"MY EYES WERE TOO HEAVY TO KEEP OPEN, BUT WAY TOO CURIOUS TO CLOSE."
—CHARLOTTE

"COURAGE. KINDNESS. FRIENDSHIP. CHARACTER. THESE ARE THE QUALITIES THAT DEFINE US AS HUMAN BEINGS, AND PROPEL US, ON OCCASION, TO GREATNESS." —MR. TUSHMAN

"IT'S LIKE THE EXTINCTION OF THE DINOSAURS. A METEOR HITS YOUR HEART
AND CHANGES EVERYTHING FOREVER. BUT YOU'RE STILL HERE."
—SUMMER

"AND I WAS LIKE, CONFORMING TO STANDARD? USUAL? TYPICAL? EXPECTED? UGH! WHO THE HECK WANTS TO BE EXPECTED ANYWAY?" —JACK

"IT'S LIKE PEOPLE YOU SEE SOMETIMES, AND YOU CAN'T IMAGINE WHAT IT WOULD BE LIKE TO BE THAT PERSON. . . . I KNOW THAT I'M THAT PERSON TO OTHER PEOPLE. . . . TO ME, THOUGH, I'M JUST ME. AN ORDINARY KID."

—AUGGIE

"MAY HE WALK FOREVER TALL IN THE GARDEN OF GOD."

—INSCRIPTION ON THE TOMB OF JULIAN AUGUSTE BAUMIER

"PLAY THE TILES YOU GET!" —GRANDMA NELLY

"WHEN GIVEN THE CHOICE BETWEEN BEING RIGHT OR BEING KIND, CHOOSE KIND." —DR. WAYNE W. DYER

"AND WHEN GOOD FRIENDS NEED US, WE DO WHAT WE CAN TO HELP THEM, RIGHT? WE CAN'T JUST BE FRIENDS WHEN IT'S CONVENIENT. GOOD FRIENDSHIPS ARE WORTH A LITTLE EXTRA EFFORT!" —CHRISTOPHER'S MOM

"IT'S A SCIENTIFIC FACT, THE WORLD IS NICER
TO POLITE PEOPLE."—MR. BROWNE

"WE'RE ALL MADE OF STARDUST!"
—SUMMER

"KINDNESS IS A LANGUAGE THE DEAF CAN HEAR AND THE BLIND CAN SEE."
—MARK TWAIN

"KINDNESS CAN SPREAD FROM PERSON TO PERSON LIKE GLITTER. . . .
YOU CAN'T SHAKE IT OFF YOU. YOU PASS IT ON TO THE NEXT PERSON. ITS
SPARKLING REMNANTS LINGER FOR DAYS. AND FOR EACH TINY DOT YOU FIND,
YOU KNOW THAT A HUNDRED MORE HAVE SEEMINGLY VANISHED. BUT WHERE
DID THEY GO? WHAT HAPPENS TO ALL THAT GLITTER? . . . ONCE IT'S OUT OF
THE BOTTLE, THERE'S JUST NO WAY OF PUTTING IT BACK." —MR. BROWNE

"ALWAYS BE ON THE LOOKOUT FOR THE PRESENCE OF WONDER."
—E. B. WHITE

"MAYBE IT IS A LOTTERY, BUT THE UNIVERSE MAKES IT ALL EVEN OUT IN THE END. THE UNIVERSE TAKES CARE OF ALL ITS BIRDS." —JUSTIN

"I THINK THERE SHOULD BE A RULE THAT EVERYONE IN THE WORLD SHOULD GET A STANDING OVATION AT LEAST ONCE IN THEIR LIVES." —AUGGIE

THIS IS A BORZOI BOOK PUBLISHED BY
ALFRED A. KNOPF

Text copyright © 2015 by R. J. Palacio
Illustrations copyright © 2015 by R. J. Palacio,
Tad Carpenter, and Shutterstock

All rights reserved. Published in the United States by
Alfred A. Knopf, an imprint of
Random House Children's Books, a division of Random House LLC,
a Penguin Random House Company, New York.

Knopf, Borzoi Books, and the colophon are
registered trademarks of Random House LLC.

The quotations that appear herein were originally published in:
Wonder copyright © 2012 by R. J. Palacio
The Julian Chapter copyright © 2014 by R. J. Palacio
365 Days of Wonder copyright © 2014 by R. J. Palacio
Pluto copyright © 2015 by R. J. Palacio

ISBN 978-0-553-49907-0

Manufactured in China

July 2015
10 9 8 7 6 5 4 3 2 1